PUFFIN BOOKS
UK | USA | Canada | Ireland | Australia
India | New Zealand | South Africa

Puffin Books is part of the Penguin Random House group of companies
whose addresses can be found at global.penguinrandomhouse.com.

www.penguin.co.uk   www.puffin.co.uk   www.ladybird.co.uk

Penguin
Random House
UK

First published in Great Britain 2023
003
Copyright © Frederick Warne & Co. Ltd, 2023
Peter Rabbit™ & Beatrix Potter™ Frederick Warne & Co.
Frederick Warne & Co. is the owner of all rights, copyrights and
trademarks in the Beatrix Potter character names and illustrations

Printed in China

The authorized representative in the EEA is Penguin Random House Ireland,
Morrison Chambers, 32 Nassau Street, Dublin D02 YH68

A CIP catalogue record for this book is available from the British Library

978-0-241-60647-6

All correspondence to:
Puffin Books, Penguin Random House Children's
One Embassy Gardens, 8 Viaduct Gardens, London SW11 7BW

Welcome TO THE WORLD, my TINY ONE.

Our DAYS **TOGETHER** have JUST begun.

You've
BROUGHT JOY,
laughter

and a
love so
STRONG-

forever
BY
your
SIDE

IS
WHERE
I
belong.

Come
RAIN OR
shine,

I know
THIS MUCH
IS
true...

I cherish ALL the MOMENTS

that

I HAVE

WITH *you.*

On

QUIET

DAYS,

WE'LL

watch

THE
clouds
DRIFT
ON *by.*

On
busy
DAYS,
WE'LL
play

beneath

A

RAINBOW

sky.

WITH *your* PAW IN *mine,*

I'LL *see*
THE
WORLD
anew...

AND I
cannot
WAIT

TO
share
IT ALL
with
YOU.

No
matter
WHERE

you
GO...

OR *how* FAR

you

ROAM...

IN MY
loving
ARMS

YOU'LL
always
FIND
your
HOME.